Starlight Songs

and other stories

*Hodder
Children's
Books*

A division of Hachette Children's Books

How to make your Felicity wishes

WISH

With this book comes an extra special wish
for you and your best friend.
Hold the book together at each end and
both close your eyes.
Wriggle your noses and think of a
number under ten.

Open your eyes, whisper the numbers you
thought of to each other.
Add these numbers together. This is your

Magic Number.

you

best friend

Place your little finger
on the stars, and say your magic number
out loud together. Now make your wish
quietly to yourselves. And maybe, one day,
your wish might just come true.

Love *felicity* x

For the real Katey Woo,
a fairy sister. x

Felicity Wishes

FELICITY WISHES
Felicity Wishes © 2000 Emma Thomson
Licensed by White Lion Publishing

Text and Illustrations © 2007 Emma Thomson

First published in Great Britain in 2007 by Hodder Children's Books

The right of Emma Thomson to be identified as the author and illustrator of this work has
been asserted by her in accordance with the Copyright, Designs and Patents Act 1988.

1

A Catalogue record for this book is available from the British Library.

ISBN: 9 780 34091749 7

Printed in the UK by CPI Bookmarque, Croydon, CRO 4TD

The paper and board used in this paperback by Hodder Children's Books are natural recyclable
products made from wood grown in sustainable forests. The manufacturing processes
conform to the environmental regulations of the country of origin.

Hodder Children's Books
A division of Hachette Children's Books, 338 Euston Road, London NW1 3BH

CONTENTS

Starlight Songs

Magical Moment

Sensational Surprise

Starlight Songs

Felicity Wishes woke with a start, roused from her dream by the clatter of her garden gate and the bang of her letter box. She fluttered to the window just in time to see the Post Fairy fly away in a flurry, looking very tired and weighed down with letters for so early in the morning.

What could it be? thought Felicity, who loved to receive letters. "Oh, it could be a letter from Bea. I haven't heard from her in ages!" she said excitedly. Bea was Felicity's penfriend, ever since Felicity had met her on a magical holiday to Petal Mountain.

Felicity flew down the stairs as fast as she could, stopping so quickly she banged the tip of her crown against the front door!

"Oh," she said rather disappointedly as she picked the letter up from her sparkly pink doormat. It wasn't from Bea at all, but had the School of Nine Wishes stamped across the front. Felicity opened the letter, a little puzzled.

"It's not time for an end-of-term report, and sports day isn't for months yet," she thought.

As Felicity read the letter she became more and more down-hearted.

Dear Fairy,

This term you are required to take part in work experience in order to prepare you for Fairy World. You should think carefully before choosing your place of employment and your choice should reflect your ideal future career. If you are unsure of what you wish to be when you leave school you will be allocated a placement that will take into consideration your strengths as a student. Please report to my office in one week, having chosen and contacted your employer.

Good luck!

Fairy Godmother

Felicity's best friends, Holly, Polly, Daisy and Winnie, all knew exactly what they wanted to be after graduating, but Felicity still had no idea. She phoned her fairy friends and arranged to meet them in their favourite café, Sparkles, hoping that they could help her find a fun place to work.

Felicity was the first to arrive at the café and ordered herself an extra-large hot chocolate with a tower of cream on top, dotted with pink marshmallows, to try and raise her drooping wings. She didn't have long to wait before Holly, Polly, Daisy and Winnie came fluttering through the door in a cloud of excitement.

"I phoned them the second I got the letter and they said they'd love to have me after we helped them so much with the newspaper article," Daisy enthused.

Felicity guessed that Daisy, who wanted to become a Blossom Fairy, was talking about Roots 'n' Shoots, the garden centre in Little Blossoming.

"It's just perfect for me – I can look after the flowers and learn more about different varieties while I work. I can't wait!"

As the fairies settled into the chairs around Felicity they were all too excited to notice how unhappy she looked.

"Felicity, guess what?" Winnie beamed. "I called the Land of Pink theme park first thing this morning. They said they would love me to join them for work experience, after I helped them design the park. Isn't that great?"

"Well done, Winnie. That's fantastic

news," smiled Felicity, feeling very happy for her friend.

"And the Bloomfield Academy for Christmas Tree Fairies said I could join their programme for a week," Holly said, teetering on the edge of her seat, barely able to contain her excitement. "It's going to be so much fun!"

Felicity smiled, truly happy that her friends had found such suitable placements so quickly. Just then Bertie, Felicity's little blue bird, jumped up and down on her shoulder and pointed his beak towards Polly, who was slumped in an armchair, not looking very happy at all.

"Polly, whatever is the matter?" Felicity asked as all four friends noticed Polly's sad face at the same time.

"Well," Polly sniffed, large pearly tears gathering in her eyes, "I phoned the Tooth Fairy Agency this morning and they said they'd love to have me but I would have to fulfil a simple list of requirements. I thought I knew everything about being a Tooth Fairy, but they've added a new rule."

By now the tears were cascading down Polly's cheeks and making her skirt very wet. Felicity fluttered to her friend's side and put an arm around Polly's shoulders.

"I have to be able to sing a magical lullaby to send people back to sleep if they wake up while I'm gathering teeth," she sobbed.

Felicity smiled. "But you have a beautiful singing voice, Polly; you'll be able to do that easily."

Holly, Daisy and Winnie agreed with Felicity. Polly was the cleverest fairy they knew and she could do anything she put her mind to.

"No, I can't," Polly cried. "It has to be sung along to music and I can't play any musical instruments at all. It's hopeless!"

"What happens if you sing without music?" Daisy asked tentatively.

"Instead of sending someone to sleep, you wake them up!" Polly shrieked.

"I know!" said Holly, thinking out loud. "Why don't you ask one of the fairies from music class to help you out?"

"I would, but they're all away at music

camp on work experience. Haven't you noticed how quiet school has been this week?" sobbed Polly even more loudly.

Felicity, who never liked to see any of her friends upset, sat deep in concentration, trying to think of a way to solve Polly's problem. Suddenly, she beamed. "Don't worry, Polly, I think I know what we can do. It might take some time, but it could be the answer."

"But there's only a week until I have to perform my lullaby in front of the agency interviewers," Polly called after Felicity, as her friend swallowed the last of her hot chocolate and fluttered out of the café without another word.

* * *

Felicity flew straight home and immediately started leafing through the latest issue of *Fairy Girl*, her favourite magazine.

"That's it! Just what I'm looking for!"

she said aloud, pointing her wand at an advertisement.

PSYCHIC FAIRY
Call 0973

Subscribe today

Piano Lessons
Want to perform your favourite tunes for your friends? Or join a band and become the next Suzi Sparkle? For piano lessons call Miss Katy Woo, ready to help you.

Felicity pulled out her pink mobile phone and started dialling. Miss Woo was very understanding when Felicity explained the situation and said that although she didn't usually teach on Sundays she would make an exception for Felicity and start teaching her the next morning.

* * *

Felicity was up bright and early the next day, dusting off the brand-new golden piano that had sat in her attic, unused, unseen and still in its original packaging since the previous year! Felicity was always trying out new hobbies and last year had decided that she wanted to learn a musical instrument. But by the time the piano had arrived Felicity had moved on to something new – knitting wand warmers!

Right on time the doorbell rang and Felicity ran to greet the beautiful Miss Woo, who stood smiling with long dark hair and sparkling eyes.

"Hello, you must be Felicity. Oh, it's so nice to meet you. I really hope I can help you in time for Polly's audition. Did you say the lullaby has to send people to sleep if they wake up? I've never heard of such a thing!"

Felicity smiled at the friendly fairy.

"Yes, it's a new rule. Polly's really worried she won't be able to do it so I hope I can help her."

"What's the song?" asked Miss Woo, opening up her music books.

"It's Polly's favourite – 'Starlight Song' – she wrote it for the school play last year."

After two hours of hard concentration, which was not easy

for Felicity, Miss Woo had taught her all the basic things she needed to know to be a pianist. Felicity wasn't sure she would be able to remember all she had been taught, but tried very hard for Polly's sake. By the time the lesson was over she could just about play 'Twinkle Twinkle Little Star' with her right hand, and although it wasn't anywhere near as complicated as the lullaby, Felicity knew it was a start.

"Thank you so much, Miss Woo. I really don't know what I would have done without you," Felicity said as she showed her teacher to the door.

"It's no trouble, Felicity, I'm glad to help! And please, call me Katy!"

* * *

After Katy had gone, Felicity went straight back to the piano and carried on practising until the phone rang an hour later. She let her answerphone cut in.

"Hello, I'm sorry I can't come to the phone right now, but please leave a sparkling message after the beep and I'll get right back to you."

"Felicity, where are you? It's Winnie," came the voice.

As soon as Felicity heard it was Winnie, she ran to the phone and picked it up. "Sorry Winnie, I was just busy practising my, ummm, dance routine for Suzi Sparkle's new song," Felicity gushed, deciding to keep her plan a surprise.

"That's OK," Winnie replied, sounding a little confused. "We're all going to the café and wondered if you wanted to come."

"Thank you, but no, I really must get back to practising. Bye!"

Felicity loved meeting her friends, but right now practising the piano really was more important.

✳ ✳ ✳

For the rest of the week, Felicity had a piano lesson each afternoon straight after school and practised all night. By Wednesday, Miss Fossil had told her off for rushing her history homework, by Thursday Miss Meandering was very cross that Felicity hadn't finished her geography assignment, but on Friday Miss Quaver was extremely pleased at the huge progress Felicity had made with her musical theory.

That afternoon, Felicity ran to the gate to meet her friends as they left school.

"Felicity, where have you been? We've hardly seen you all week!" Daisy rushed up to Felicity and gave her a big hug.

"I've been a bit busy, ummm, doing something," Felicity stuttered, feeling awful that she couldn't tell her friends the whole truth. "What time is your interview tomorrow?" she asked Polly.

"At ten in the morning, but it's pointless going. I've practised all week long trying to send fairies to sleep with various instruments, but the  recorder made them more wide awake than ever, the trumpet set them off giggling, and the tambourine sent them flying sky high! What am I going to do? I can't sing 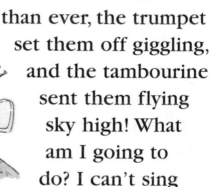 unaccompanied – the lullaby won't work."

"It will all be OK, Poll. Trust me! I'll see you outside the agency tomorrow at 9.45," said Felicity as she turned to fly home, leaving behind four very puzzled fairy faces.

* * *

The next morning there was a loud knock on Felicity's front door.

"Huh! What's going on? Oh no, it's 9.45 already!" Felicity shrieked as she quickly scooped up her crown from the piano where it had fallen off her head. Felicity had spent the whole night practising and must have fallen asleep while she was doing it!

"I'm coming, I'm coming!" she called, grabbing her music and rushing to the front door.

Daisy and Winnie were standing outside looking very flustered. "Polly's getting really worried," Daisy puffed.

"We flew here from the agency to see where you'd got to," Winnie panted. "You go ahead and we'll catch you up."

Felicity flew off as fast as she could, checking her pink watch every few seconds as it ticked closer and closer towards 10 a.m. She landed with a fairy-like thump next to Polly and Holly, who looked very relieved to see Felicity. Felicity was not so happy, though. She had spent all night trying to get the final bar of the lullaby right, but she just hadn't been able to manage the tricky chord sequence and couldn't remember if she had mastered it or not.

"Quick! We've got to get inside," Polly said, grabbing Felicity's arm and leading her in. "What's your plan, Felicity?"

"I'm going to play the piano while you sing! I've been learning all week, just for you," Felicity told her friend with a shaky smile, deciding it would be better not to tell Polly that she couldn't play it perfectly.

Polly gave Felicity the biggest, most radiant smile she had ever seen. They crashed through the door to the big white room where Polly's audition was to be held.

Inside, at least fifteen very stern-looking fairies sat behind a long table. Felicity scanned their faces, and not one was smiling.

"Name?" demanded a fairy in half-moon glasses, and grey hair in a tight bun perched right in the middle of her head.

"Urm, Polly and this is, urm, Felicity, who'll be playing the piano for me," said Polly.

"And how do you suppose you will take a piano with you while you are collecting teeth?" asked the stern fairy, peering over the top of her spectacles while the others all stared at the two nervous fairies.

Polly looked desperately at Felicity.

"I'm going to record my accompaniment, so Polly can take it

with her and sing along," Felicity
replied, her wings shaking.

The interviewing fairy tutted and
looked back down at the papers on

her desk. "Very well, begin!"

Felicity settled herself at the piano and tried to hold her shaking fingers steady as she began to play.

The next thing she knew, she was being poked in the side by something very pointy and wand-like.

"Huh, where am I?" she asked, sitting up and straightening her crown as she realized she had fallen asleep at the piano again! "Oh, no! I'm so sorry, Polly. I've ruined everything! I must have been so tired from practising all night that I fell asleep." Felicity felt absolutely terrible as she looked at Polly, only to see a smile spreading over her friend's face.

"It's OK, Felicity – you sent yourself to sleep by playing the lullaby!" Polly beamed. "Look!" And she pointed towards the table of fairies at the front of the room. They were all spread across it, snoring in unison!

Felicity began to giggle as she realized what had happened. "So, it went OK? It worked?"

"Yes! You were great and played every note perfectly!" Polly said, giving her friend a big hug.

Together they went to wake up the examining fairies. Polly shook the shoulder of the fairy who had questioned her at the start.

"Oh, yes. Very well done. You've passed. Welcome to the Tooth Fairy Agency, keeping your teeth safe!" the fairy garbled as she sat up and smoothed the crumpled page in front of her.

Felicity and Polly left the room arm in arm, only to find Holly, Winnie and Daisy, who had been secretly listening from outside the room, curled up on the floor, fast asleep!

Magical Moment

Felicity Wishes and her friends were sharing some berry biscuits during their lunch hour and chatting about their work experience placements. Felicity wasn't as excited as the other fairies: unlike her friends, she had no idea what sort of fairy she wanted to be when she left the School of Nine Wishes. As a result, choosing somewhere that reflected her ideal future career was proving very difficult.

"Don't worry, Felicity, Fairy Godmother said she would find a placement for anyone who couldn't decide," Winnie reminded her friend.

"Yes, but what if Fairy Godmother chooses something really bad?" Felicity groaned. "Like cleaning toilets!"

"Don't be silly, Felicity," Polly reasoned. "In the letter, Fairy Godmother said she would allocate you a placement that will take into consideration your strengths as a student." Polly recited the letter almost perfectly.

"But what are my strengths as a student? I never listen in class and I always hand in my homework late. In geography, I don't know where any countries are on the map, in history, I don't know what happened last century, and my science experiments always go wrong!"

Felicity's friends all tried to think of something nice they could say, but it was true that although she was a great friend and tried very hard, she didn't do all that well at school.

"You've really improved in music since you learnt the piano," Daisy said encouragingly. "Miss Quaver was impressed."

Just then there was an announcement over the school tannoy system: "Would Felicity Wishes please report to Fairy Godmother's office immediately," came the nasal voice, booming through the school hall.

"Wish me luck," Felicity said to her friends, her wings all a-quiver.

"Good luck!" she heard them chorus behind her.

She fluttered along the corridor leading to Fairy Godmother's office, tapped lightly on the door and waited for the faint "come in" before entering the vast room.

One of the walls was filled with

filing cabinets reaching right up to the ceiling. Each drawer was bulging with notes on every student in the school. Fairy Godmother was hovering right at the top of one cabinet, her crown brushing the ceiling as she pulled out a huge file.

Felicity blushed as she realized that all her reports would be inside, but was pleased to see the folder was pink and glittery! Fairy Godmother fluttered to the ground and took her seat behind a huge old desk.

"Right, Felicity, let's have a look. What is your favourite subject?" Fairy Godmother asked, motioning for her to sit down.

"Well," Felicity replied thoughtfully, "I love cooking and dancing. I recently learnt to play the piano to help my best friend and since then I've really enjoyed music."

"Yes, yes, I see. Miss Quaver seems

to think you've made a great improvement," Fairy Godmother agreed, reading Felicity's most recent report. "So how would you feel about a job that involves music?"

Felicity instantly started to brighten up and grinned across the desk. "That would be fantastic – do you really think I could? I'd love to do something with music. I love playing the piano and I practise all the time and even though I started learning just to help Polly, I've carried on having lessons because I enjoy them so much and…"

Felicity got carried away talking about her new love for the piano.

Fairy Godmother chuckled. "I'm sure we could find you something. In fact, have you ever been to the opera?"

"No, I haven't, but I'd love to go. Thank you," Felicity replied, unsure why Fairy Godmother was asking her to the opera instead of organizing her work experience.

"How about I give my friend Madame Maria Soprana a ring?" Fairy Godmother continued. "She owns the local opera house in Little Blossoming."

"Wow, that would be great!" Felicity really liked the idea of working in an opera house, listening to music all night long.

Fairy Godmother smiled, and closed Felicity's file.

* * *

Holly, Daisy, Winnie and Polly were all very pleased for Felicity when she told them her news.

"I can't wait!" Felicity gushed to her

friends as they sat in Sparkles café that evening. "Can you imagine sitting listening to opera all night long, for a job?"

"I don't think that's all you'll do!" Polly suggested sensibly. "Maybe you'll be given a job selling tickets, or showing fairies to their seats, or taking ice cream round during the interval."

Felicity let out a long moan. She really hoped not! She'd once worked at the cinema for a day, but she'd been so busy making friends with everyone, she hadn't managed to show them to their seats before the film started – then she'd tripped in the dark and sent popcorn and fizzy pop flying everywhere – then she'd eaten all the ice cream she was supposed to be selling – and to top it all off she was sick all over aisle G!

She reconsidered. "Maybe the opera won't be the best job in the world."

"It'll be fine! I'm sure you'll get to see the opera, and you'll make lots of new friends," Holly reassured Felicity. "And there are hundreds of different jobs in the opera house that you could end up doing!"

* * *

By the time the following week arrived, Felicity had prepared herself in every way she could. She'd spent three lunchtimes in the library (with a little help from Polly), finding books on the beginning of opera in Fairy World, hundreds of years ago;

spent hours at home studying the technical terms for different types of songs; and promised herself that she would keep conversations with members of the audience to a minimum and not eat any ice cream whatsoever.

* * *

On her first morning, Felicity fluttered into the opera house feeling very nervous. She looked around in awe at the marble pillars, gold ceiling and plush red carpet. Reminding herself why she was there, she went over to the desk, where a fairy was engrossed in the latest issue of *Fairy Girl*. Felicity had to clear her throat several times before the fairy looked up.

"Can I help you?" she asked Felicity, without even so much as a hint of welcome on her face.

"Yes, please, I was told to ask for Madame Maria Soprana. I'm Felicity Wishes, here on work experience,"

Felicity replied with her best smile.

"Just one moment." The Reception Fairy picked up her telephone, dialled a short code, and told someone there was a fairy in the lobby.

Moments later a very flustered-looking fairy came fluttering ungracefully into the lobby and stopped in front of Felicity.

"I'm Carmeena. Madame Soprana is in a meeting at the moment and we're a few staff down backstage, so she's asked me to show you round and give you a few jobs to do. Follow me!" the flustered fairy gabbled.

Felicity thought that working back-stage at the opera sounded ever so exciting. She followed the fairy down several corridors and on to the stage.

"Right, there's a broom, a bucket and a mop over there. You need to sweep the stage then wash it, but don't make the water too bubbly or it gets slippery

and the cast will fall over when they
dance. Then you need to arrange all
the props for the first scene tonight,
there's a diagram over there and the
props are over there," Carmeena said,
pointing all around the huge area
behind the stage. "Then you need to
oil the pulley system for the curtains
and make sure it works smoothly, then
close the curtains so no one can see
the stage. Then tidy and clean all the
dressing rooms, fill them with fresh
flowers and arrange the costumes on

the rails in the order they will be worn. Then make sure all the orchestra's instruments are in the right places and the music is in the right order. Then report back to me. OK?"

Felicity's head was buzzing at the long list of jobs and already she had started to forget some of them.

"Yes, OK, I think," she replied uncertainly.

"I've got a million and one things to do, but I'll be around." And Carmeena zoomed off behind the stage.

Trying as hard as she could to remember everything, Felicity started to sweep the stage. She really hadn't thought work experience would be this hard! But it was exciting to stand on the stage and look out at all the seats, pretending she was the star of the opera.

By lunchtime, Felicity had hardly done any of the jobs; by teatime she was still behind and getting very, very tired. She pushed open the door of the lead fairy's dressing room with her foot as she struggled to hold the masses of flowers she had to arrange.

The dressing room was even bigger than Felicity's bedroom and filled with beautiful posters of fairies from operas around the world and letters from adoring fans. Felicity arranged the flowers into vases, then picked up a crumpled dress from the floor.

"Oh!" she exclaimed as she saw how beautiful it was. It was made of silk and velvet, lace and ribbons, sequins and beads, flowers and bows. The cream silk flowed to the ground, covering Felicity's toes as she held it up against herself. Gold patterns were embroidered into the bodice and tiny gold butterflies danced on the back. Felicity touched the fragile, intricate detail and longed to try the dress on.

"No one will see me," she thought to herself. "I'll just put it on for a second and take it off again straight away!"

Carefully, she stepped into the dress and buttoned it up. She moved in front of the full-length mirror and couldn't believe her eyes: she looked amazing.

The dress had clearly been made many decades ago, but it suited her perfectly. It was almost as if the dress had been made for Felicity...

Felicity had been working hard all day and her tiny fairy feet were throbbing from standing up for so long. Out of the corner of her eye, she saw a beautiful chaise longue, covered with cushions of every shape and size.

"Surely no one would mind if I just rested for a few minutes before getting on with the rest of my jobs?" thought Felicity as she collapsed in a heap on the soft cushions.

But the next thing she knew, she was woken by a knock on the door. A tiny fairy poked her head round, looking shy when she realized that Felicity was in there.

"I'm so sorry to disturb you! I was just going to sweep up in here, but I'll come back later!"

"You aren't disturbing me," Felicity stuttered, sitting upright, her cheeks turning from pink to purple with embarrassment. "Erm, I was going to sweep in here, but if you'd like to, I'll pop out for a minute and leave you to it!" she said, fluttering out of the door before the little fairy had a chance to say anything about her dress.

The little fairy looked puzzled as the door closed.

* * *

As Felicity stood in the corridor, desperately trying to unbutton the dress before anyone else caught her wearing one of the costumes, she could hear voices approaching... "Oh, no! I can't let them see me in this dress or I could be in terrible trouble!" thought Felicity. "And imagine what Fairy Godmother would say if I was sacked from my work experience!"

Felicity quickly made her way through winding corridors, double doors and heavy curtains, in the opposite direction of the voices until she found herself backstage, and in the middle of an opera! She had never seen a real-life opera before and was awestruck at the theatrics of it all – the beautiful costumes, the dramatic lighting and the most magnificent voices she had ever heard, filling the stage.

Peeping through the curtains, Felicity

saw that the fairies in the audience
were wearing dresses of every colour
of the rainbow, sparkling with glitter
and gems. They all had graceful hair-
styles, often with their hair piled in
curls on top of their heads – nothing
like Felicity had ever seen before! It
was as if she had been magically
transformed back in time.

Felicity stopped to wonder at these
strange fairies, who looked as if they
had stepped right out of a history

book! In fact, the longer Felicity thought about it the more she noticed how odd her surroundings were. The opera house didn't look quite like it had that morning – Felicity was sure that there was proper lighting and not candles, plastic seats instead of velvet ones, and she couldn't see the ice cream ushers anywhere!

As the opera finished, the audience emptied out and the opera fairies went to their dressing rooms, Felicity also noticed that they spoke using very long words, and not one of them seemed to have a mobile phone! One of them was even talking about leaving in her horse-drawn carriage!

Felicity was so busy looking around the theatre, she hadn't noticed that the tiny fairy from the dressing room had reappeared and started to sweep the stage.

"Hello again!" said the little fairy.

"My name's Poppy. Are you a singer?"

"No!" laughed Felicity, still trying to hide her dress. "I really like singing, but I'd never be good enough to perform on stage."

"Don't say that!" Poppy encouraged. "I am sure you will be, one day!"

Felicity smiled at her new friend and came out from behind the curtain.

"Wow! I've never seen a wand like yours before," Poppy said wistfully, looking at Felicity's silver-starred wand.

"And I've never seen one like yours either!" said Felicity, admiring Poppy's ornate golden wand. "I would be at the height of fashion at the School of Nine Wishes with a wand like that."

"I know, why don't we swap wands?" the little fairy suggested, pleased to be able to make her new friend happy.

Felicity swapped her wand without a moment's thought. She was busy swooshing and swishing with her new

wand when she heard a loud banging
noise coming from the dressing rooms.

"Whatever could that be?" said
Felicity to Poppy. "I wonder if I left a
window open when I was in there
earlier?"

Felicity reluctantly left Poppy
sweeping the stage and went to
investigate. But when she got to the
lead fairy's dressing room, the window
was closed! She was still feeling rather

sleepy and the lure of the chaise longue was too much for her again. It wasn't long before she was snoring softly.

This time, Felicity was woken up by an even louder bang that sounded like the dressing-room door. Felicity ran to let in the fairy outside.

"Oh, hello, I see you like my dress!" a fairy said in a sing-song voice. Felicity saw that she was wearing modern clothes! "I hate to ask you to take it off, but I've got to wear it in a minute."

Felicity blushed brighter than she ever had blushed before. "I'm so sorry, I've been so busy today I… think… I fell asleep, I just wanted to see what it looked like, it's so lovely and…" Her voice trailed off as she saw the fairy smiling.

"It's OK, don't worry, I don't mind at all. I'm Latilla – I play the lead in the opera. Thank you for cleaning my room, it looks lovely."

Felicity smiled and quickly slipped out of the dress, said goodbye and left Latilla to get changed. Outside she caught sight of Carmeena, who told her the day's work was done and the opera was about to start. She gave Felicity a sparkling front row ticket to watch that evening's performance.

That night, as Latilla was ending the opera with a beautiful solo, Felicity's eyes filled with gleaming tears. She reached into her pocket for a handkerchief, but instead felt something hard and pointy. It was Poppy's wand! A broad smile filled Felicity's face.

"My trip back in time was real, after all!" she gasped, as the curtains closed.

It is always fun
making new friends

wherever they are from!

Sensational Surprise

It was nearly the end of work experience for Felicity and her friends. Polly had collected more than a hundred teeth, working alongside six other fairies at the Tooth Fairy Agency. Joining in with lessons at the Christmas Tree Fairy Academy, Holly had learnt how to balance on the top of a Christmas tree and twirl at the same time. Winnie had been in charge of every ride in the Land of Pink theme park, and Daisy had learnt all about twenty brand-new varieties of plants at the Roots 'n' Shoots garden centre.

Meanwhile, Felicity had spent the week working at the opera house in Little Blossoming. By day she scrubbed the floors, arranged the flowers and hung up the costumes, but by night she was drawn into a whole new world as she watched the opera from her front row seat, learning all the words and dance moves by heart.

Each fairy in the opera knew her part inside out, and performed with so much sparkle that Felicity began to wish she could join the opera company. In fact, one night she'd got so carried away, she started to sing along with the lead fairy – until the person sitting next to her poked Felicity with her wand and asked her very politely to be quiet!

Felicity had enjoyed her work

experience so much that she'd offered to work on the forthcoming Saturday as well. She couldn't wait until the evening, when all her fairy friends would join her to watch the performance.

Felicity was busy dusting the lead fairy's dressing room when she heard a commotion outside the door. "I can't, it's stuck!" she heard a fairy wail.

"You have to do something! You're on in half an hour!" another fairy replied.

Felicity wondered what on earth was going on and fluttered to the door just as it crashed open. Latilla, the lead fairy, came swishing through the door in a fluster with her foot stuck behind her head, followed by Maria Soprana, the owner of the opera house. Felicity looked at her in shock, wondering what on earth could have happened.

"I over-stretched in my yoga class," Latilla explained, reading the puzzled expression on Felicity's face, "and now my foot's stuck and I can't move it at all! And the opera starts in half an hour!" she cried.

Felicity saw the panic in Latilla's eyes and offered to help. "Maybe if I pull this way and you bend this way," she said to Latilla, "we might be able to move it together."

"I'll try anything, thank you,' Latilla said gratefully.

Felicity set about trying to pull Latilla's right foot out from behind her left ear, heaving with all her might in every way she could think of, while trying not to hurt the fairy.

"Oh, dear," Felicity said, out of breath, as she stopped pulling. "I really do think it is stuck!"

"I know!" wailed Latilla even louder. "I'll have to go back to the yoga teacher to get it sorted out!"

Felicity looked at Madame Maria, sitting on a chair in the corner of the room with her head in her hands.

"What are we going to do?" the fairy sobbed. "The seats are already filling up, it's Saturday night and we're fully booked, but no one else knows the

part as well as Latilla. Her understudy
is at home with a sore throat!"

Felicity looked down at the ground.
Quietly, she said, "Urm, I, urm, well, I've
watched the opera every night this
week, and I, urm, I know all the words
and I can remember all the dance
steps, but I, urm, I can't sing and I'm
really not good at performing. I get so
nervous, in fact, I have stage fright, but

I, urm, want to help in any way I can."

Latilla and Madame Maria looked at Felicity in wonder.

"So you could fill in for Latilla?" Madame Maria asked, suddenly seeming perkier.

"Well, I was just thinking of all the fairies who have come to see the opera tonight and how disappointed they would be if it was cancelled, and I've never performed such a huge role on stage but I guess I could give it a go if I try to control my nerves," Felicity replied, feeling far from confident.

Latilla hopped up to her and gave her a very awkward hug.

"But I really can't sing at all well, and nowhere near as good as you, Latilla. What if all the fairies in the audience complain?" Felicity said worriedly.

"I know!" Madame Maria said,

excited now. "Felicity, we can turn off your microphone and you can mime, and Latilla can sit behind stage with another microphone, singing all the songs. No one will know!"

It seemed like the perfect solution. Felicity started to become more confident as she slipped on Latilla's dress and the make-up fairies buzzed around her.

With only five minutes left until the opera began, Felicity was still nervous, but she was also a bit excited! Just then she remembered she had told Holly, Polly, Winnie and Daisy to meet her outside the opera house ten minutes before the start! She grabbed her mobile phone and dialled Polly's number.

"Felicity, where are you?" came
Polly's answer.

"I'm sorry, you'll have to watch the
opera without me, but I'll see you
there!" Felicity said chirpily.

"Felicity, you're not making sense,"
said Polly, confused.

"I won't be sitting with you after
all," Felicity tried to explain, "but I will

be there. Look out for me! I've got to go, bye!" She hung up, hoping Polly wouldn't be too cross with her.

"Ready to go on in three minutes, Felicity?" Madame Maria called as she came fluttering back into the dressing room. "Oh!" she exclaimed as she saw Felicity in her dress. "You look wonderful – and just like Latilla!"

Felicity smiled shakily and got up to prepare herself. "Madame Maria, I've just got one question," she said quietly. "Sometimes, watching the opera, I've been so carried away by the music I've started to sing along. I'm worried that I might do the same tonight, only, well, will anyone hear me?"

"Oh, no, of course not, Felicity! Your microphone will be switched off and the music will be so loud no one will hear you at all. You can sing as loudly as you like!" Madame Maria replied happily.

Behind the stage Latilla was sitting in her chair, warming up her voice to begin.

"La la la la la la la la la. Good luck on stage, Felicity. Don't break a leg – or get one stuck behind your head!" she sang as Felicity went past.

All of Felicity's nerves returned as she climbed the steps on to the stage and positioned herself for the opening song. As the curtains slowly swooshed apart she saw Winnie, Holly, Polly and Daisy sitting in a nearby box. She gave them a tiny wave as the orchestra charged into the song, and giggled as she saw Polly's shocked expression, Daisy nearly falling off her chair and Holly and Winnie waving frantically back at their friend.

With their smiling faces in front of her, Felicity soon forgot all about her stage fright.

During the first song, Felicity

managed not to make a sound. She loved listening to Latilla's voice booming across the speakers and pretended it was her, just as everyone in the audience thought it was. She concentrated as hard as she could to move around the stage just as Latilla had and mime along in perfect time. As each song finished and a new one began, Felicity grew in confidence – and before she knew it she was singing along, very quietly at first but then more and more loudly as the opera went on.

For the final song, all the fairies in the show gathered together on stage to sing a chorus. It was just what Felicity had dreamt of doing, and she sang along at full volume. She could hear her voice blending in with the others, but knew that no one else would be able to hear her. As the other fairies on stage sang their last notes,

she finished the song by singing the final high note as loudly as she could manage, making herself dizzy with the effort!

"That's funny," Felicity thought as she finished. "I couldn't hear Latilla at all during the last song. I suppose hearing myself sing must have drowned her voice out, so I couldn't hear it!" She bowed as the audience clapped and cheered for an encore. It felt as if all her dreams were coming true!

* * *

By the time Felicity had climbed down from the stage and reached Latilla's dressing room, Holly, Polly, Winnie and Daisy were waiting for her outside the door.

"You were fantastic, Felicity!" Holly cried as she ran up to hug her friend.

"It was amazing!" Daisy beamed from behind Holly.

"I didn't know you could sing so well, Felicity. Have you been having lessons without telling us?" asked Winnie. She suspected that Felicity might have learnt to sing in secret, just like she had learnt to play the piano, and kept it a surprise.

"Felicity, you were absolutely brilliant – how did you do it?" Polly asked, as she stepped back to allow

Felicity into the dressing room.

Felicity grabbed a glass of water, because her throat was dry after so much singing, and looked at all of her friends.

"It wasn't me!" she said, watching their faces turn from happy to confused.

"Yes, it was. We saw you!" said Winnie, trying to work out what Felicity meant.

"Well, yes, it was me on stage, but I

wasn't singing. My microphone was turned off and Latilla was singing the whole time!" Felicity explained.

"Oh," said Holly, a little upset.

"So you weren't singing at all?" asked Winnie.

"Yes, I was singing, but you could only hear Latilla's voice. She was back-stage with a real microphone. I had to stand in for her, because she couldn't go on stage. It's a long story but…" Felicity stopped as she saw her friend's disappointed faces.

"We just thought…" began Polly.

"Well, we all know what we want to be when we leave school but you don't, and we thought that doing work experience at the opera house had helped you discover a new talent," continued Winnie.

"We thought you could be an Opera Fairy," finished Holly.

Felicity could see why her friends

felt so disappointed, but she was still happy with her performance. Never in a million fairy years had she ever thought she would have the confidence to get up on stage in front of all those fairies.

"I'm sorry," she said, "but I got over my stage fright and I had a really great time. And I'm so glad you came to watch me!"

Her friends all smiled as they realized how brave Felicity had been, and rushed over to give her a group hug. Then there was a knock at the door.

"Come in!" Felicity called. Madame Maria entered, followed by Latilla.

"Felicity, we have something to tell you," Madame Maria began.

"Yes, well, it's a good job you asked Madame Maria if you could sing along tonight," Latilla continued, "because my microphone failed!"

Felicity looked from Madame Maria to Latilla, confused at what they were saying.

"A fairy tripped over the microphone plugs and pulled Latilla's out. Then she plugged in yours by mistake, Felicity, so you sang the last song all on your own!" Madame Maria explained.

Felicity didn't quite understand. "So when I sang the last high note, everyone heard me?" she asked.

"Yes," Madame Maria and Latilla chorused.

"And no one complained?" Felicity asked.

"No," they replied. Felicity looked at her friends. They were all smiling broadly, happy that it had been

Felicity they'd heard singing after all, at least for some of the time. Maybe she could be an Opera Fairy after all!

"Well," said Winnie, "I think this deserves an extra-large strawberry milkshake at Sparkles café! Who's coming?"

Felicity, Holly, Polly and Daisy all shouted "Me!" as they fluttered out of the dressing room and left the opera house, where Felicity had shone like a real opera star!

"It just proves that you should never give up on your dreams," murmured Felicity happily, as they flew off into the starlit night.

When you least expect it

the unexpected can happen!

Emma Thomson's
felicity Wishes

Felicity is worried about Winnie

when she starts to act very strangely

after a trip to Bubble Island in

Crowning Cure

Crowning Cure

Felicity Wishes and her friends were in their favourite café, Sparkles, after school. They were listening to Winnie as she told them about her adventures on Bubble Island over the weekend.

"There are beautiful lagoons everywhere, with magical bubbles of every colour rising out of them!" Winnie was so excited she could hardly speak fast enough. "One lagoon in the very middle of the island was filled with a foam made of millions of miniature rainbow bubbles that smelt of strawberries!"

"Did you go swimming?" Holly asked.

"Oh, no, the water isn't safe. They say that if you swim in it you'll turn into a giant bubble and float into the sky!"

The fairies gasped.

"Has it ever happened to anyone?" Daisy asked worriedly.

"I think that's just one of the island legends. But there are lots of nasty bubbly bugs you can catch if you go too close to the water," Winnie explained.

"Well, I hope you stayed well back," Polly said. "We have an important wish-making exam in a few days."

The fairies groaned. They didn't want to be reminded of the exam Fairy Godmother had set the previous Friday.

"I'll be fine," Winnie told Polly. "I was practising all weekend."

Felicity sank back into her chair. She had been in such a rush to leave school on Friday afternoon and welome the weekend that she'd completely forgotten to make a note of the exam. She hadn't practised at all.

"What are we going to do with you, Felicity?" Polly said with a sigh, smiling at her forgetful friend.

"It's OK, Felicity, we've got four more days. Plenty of time to practise!" Daisy reassured her.

* * *

Felicity flew into school the next morning with only one thing on her mind. She'd hardly done any practice for the exam, and time was running out. She was so preoccupied with fitting everything into her busy schedule that she didn't look where she was going. She flew straight into Winnie, who toppled backwards mid-flutter and landed on the ground in a heap.

"I'm so sorry," Felicity exclaimed, quickly bending down to help Winnie up. "Are you OK?"

At first Winnie didn't answer, but just stared straight ahead of her as though nothing had happened. As Felicity took her hand, she seemed to come round from her daze and looked quizzically at her friend.

"What happened?" she asked, confused.

"I didn't look where I was going – I was thinking about the exam – and I didn't see you…" Felicity's voice trailed off as she looked at Winnie, who seemed even more puzzled.

"What exam?" Winnie asked.

"The wish-making exam, remember? Polly reminded us yesterday, and you said you'd been practising all week-end," Felicity reminded Winnie.

"Oh, oh, yes, I'd completely forgotten." Winnie stood up and dusted off her skirt. "Where are we?" she said, looking around her.

"We're at school," Felicity replied. By now she was quite worried about her friend.

"But I was at home a minute ago! I don't remember flying here at all," Winnie said with a frown.

"Maybe you were daydreaming the whole way here," Felicity suggested kindly, trying to reassure Winnie. "Sometimes I don't remember what I've done because I'm too busy thinking of something else!"

"Yes, maybe that was it." Unsure of what had happened, Winnie flew off into the school.

As soon as Felicity saw her other friends, she told them what had happened so that they could all keep an eye out for Winnie. But the next day as Felicity was going into her science lesson Holly started telling her that exactly the same thing had happened on her way into school that morning. Winnie had flown right into her!

"She didn't remember how she had got to school and she'd forgotten to bring her bag. I had to lend her my spare pen and notebook," Holly explained before Miss Sparkle came into the room and the fairies had to be quiet.

At lunchtime Felicity, Polly, Daisy, Holly and Winnie all met under the Large Oak Tree. They were happily chatting about the latest fashions in *Fairy Girl*, their favourite magazine, when Winnie abruptly stopped talking, mid-sentence. The fairies all looked at her, waiting for her to finish what she was saying, but she just sat staring straight ahead.

"Winnie, hello, Winnie?" Felicity called, waving her hand in front of her friend's face. But Winnie didn't even blink.

"What's wrong with her?" Daisy asked, as Holly started shaking Winnie's shoulder to try to rouse her.

"I don't know, but I think we should get her to the school nurse." Polly took both of Winnie's hands and pulled her to her feet.

With Polly on one side and Felicity on the other, Winnie fluttered across the playground to the nurse's office – but she was still in a dream-like state, her eyes glazed over.

The nurse helped Polly and Felicity to lie Winnie down on the sick bed, then told them to wait outside. After only a few minutes the door opened and Winnie came striding out as though nothing had happened.

"Oh!" Felicity exclaimed, jumping off her chair and rushing up to give Winnie a huge hug. "You're OK!"

"Of course I am. The nurse thinks I'm just overly worried about the exam on Friday and should get more rest. She's given me some lavender oil to help me sleep," Winnie said, holding up a tiny purple bottle.

The other fairies were not convinced, but after all the nurse knew best! They smiled at Winnie and walked with her to their next class.

Read the rest of

Emma Thomson's

felicity Wishes

Crowning Cure

to find out what's really

wrong with Winnie.

If you enjoyed this book, why not try another of these fantastic story collections?

Designer Drama

Star Surprise

Clutter Clean-out

Newspaper Nerves

Enchanted Escape

Whispering Wishes

Friends Forever

Sensational Secrets

Happy Hobbies

Wand Wishes

Party Pickle

Dancing Dreams

14

Fashion Fiasco

13

Spooky Sleepover

15

Pink Paradise

17

Dreamy Daisy

16

Spectacular Skies

18

Perfect Polly

19 Winnie's Wonderland

20 Holly's Hideaway

21 Fairy Fun

22 Starlight Songs

23 Crowning Cure

24 Fairy Fame

26 Storytelling Stars

25 Perfect Ponies

27 Glittering Giveaways

Look out for these five special editions

Summer Sunshine

Holiday Hullabaloo

Christmas Calamity

Winter Wishes

Snowy Showdown

SEE YOUR FRIENDSHIP LETTER HERE!

Write in and tell us all about your best friend, and you could see your letter published in one of the Felicity Wishes books.

Please send in your letter, including your name and age, with a stamped self-addressed envelope to:

Felicity Wishes Friendship Competition

Hodder Children's Books, 338 Euston Road, London NW1 3BH

Australian readers should write to...
Hachette Children's Books
Level 17/207 Kent Street, Sydney, NSW 2000, Australia

New Zealand readers should write to...
Hachette Children's Books
PO Box 100-749 North Shore Mail Centre, Auckland, New Zealand

Closing date is 31st December 2007

ALL ENTRIES MUST BE SIGNED BY A PARENT OR GUARDIAN.
TO BE ELIGIBLE ENTRANTS MUST BE UNDER 13 YEARS.

For full terms and conditions visit www.felicitywishes.net/terms

Friends of Felicity

My best friend in the whole wide world is my mum because when iam sad she always comes up to me and says 'are you ok' and what ever i say she always gives me a hug and says 'it will be alright' and she never tells any one, and i would do the same for her. I think a best friend shows that what ever you say they will never tell any one else.

Felicity age 12

WOULD YOU LIKE TO BE A FRIEND OF FELICITY?

Felicity Wishes has her very own website, filled with lots of sparkly fairy fun and information about Felicity Wishes and all her fairy friends.

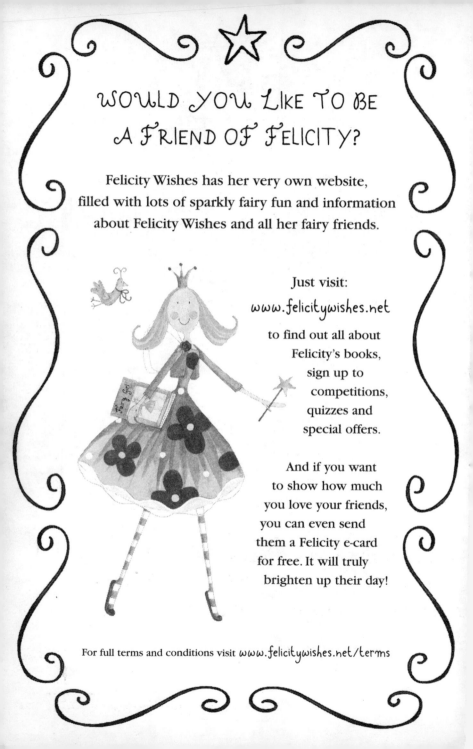

Just visit:

www.felicitywishes.net

to find out all about Felicity's books, sign up to competitions, quizzes and special offers.

And if you want to show how much you love your friends, you can even send them a Felicity e-card for free. It will truly brighten up their day!

For full terms and conditions visit www.felicitywishes.net/terms